John Williamson's Christmas in Australia

Illustrated by Mitch Vane

PENGUIN|VIKING

It's December in Australia;
Time to remember all the family.
Christmas tree – native pine,
Lights and tinsel all entwined.
Put a fairy on the top.
There's Gran and Pa and Joan and Pop.

The ham and turkey's organised.
Won't the grandkids be surprised
When Santa comes in big black boots,

In the back of Jacko's ute . . .

HO HO HO HO HO HO

It's December in Australia;
Time to remember all the family.
Gather round for a photo.
Hang on, Dad, where did Sam go?
We gotta get everyone in the picture . . .

Oh, here he is. C'mon, Sam,
Now – say 'Cheese'.

Wait a minute – Bubbles is missing.

Oh, yum yum, pig's bum – Christmas pudding.
All the ladies do the cooking.
All the men are really slack,
Slapping each other on the back.

'How ya been, Tangles? How was your year?
Might rain tomorrow. Have a cold beer.
I hear young Greg is playing fullback.
I guess he gets it all from you, Jack.'

Who's for a game of cricket?

Oh, it's December in Australia;
Time to remember all the family.
Gather round for a photo.
Hang on, Dad, where did Cher go?
We gotta get everyone in the picture . . .

Oh, here she is – C'mon, Cher,
Say 'Cheese'.

Wait a minute – Annie's not here.

Ah, me not out. Oh yes you are, Nick.
It's your bowl, Max, don't bowl too quick.
Aw, Nick has run off with the bat.
After him across the flat.

C'mon, Cub, you've had a bowl.
Give the ball to Christie.

Tom-tit, Peewee, Brookie, Sidekick,
You're on my side. Grab the bat quick.
Now he's run off with the stump.
Better give that Nick a thump.

Think I'll have another beer, Runt.

Oh, it's December in Australia;
Time to remember all the family.
Gather round for a photo.
Hang on, Dad, where did Ami go?
We gotta get everyone in the picture . . .

Oh, here she is – C'mon, Ami,
Everybody now say 'Cheese'.

Oh, wait a minute – Heddi's not here.

See the goanna up a gum tree?
He's gonna get a feed today, free,
When the campers leave the lake,
Bits of chook and chocolate cake.

It's Christmas time for him as well.
See his big long belly swell.

HEH HEH

Oh, it's December in Australia;
Time to remember all the family.
Gather round for a photo.
Hang on, Dad, where did Fox go?
Gotta get everyone in the picture . . .

Oh, here she is – C'mon now, Fox,
Everybody say 'Cheese'.
Hold it there now . . .

Oh, it's December in Australia.

To my wife, Meg, who brought this song alive as a book originally.
For me it celebrates the wonderful advantages of Christmas in summer. JW

For Deb & the Dillons & their dear smiley Jessy. MV

VIKING

Published by the Penguin Group
Penguin Group (Australia)
707 Collins Street, Melbourne, Victoria 3008, Australia
(a division of Penguin Australia Pty Ltd)
Penguin Group (USA) Inc.
375 Hudson Street, New York, New York 10014, USA
Penguin Group (Canada)
90 Eglinton Avenue East, Suite 700, Toronto, Canada ON M4P 2Y3
(a division of Penguin Canada Books Inc.)
Penguin Books Ltd
80 Strand, London WC2R 0RL England
Penguin Ireland
25 St Stephen's Green, Dublin 2, Ireland
(a division of Penguin Books Ltd)
Penguin Books India Pvt Ltd
11 Community Centre, Panchsheel Park, New Delhi – 110 017, India
Penguin Group (NZ)
67 Apollo Drive, Rosedale, Auckland 0632, New Zealand
(a division of Penguin New Zealand Pty Ltd)
Penguin Books (South Africa) (Pty) Ltd, Rosebank Office Park, Block D,
181 Jan Smuts Avenue, Parktown North, Johannesburg, 2196, South Africa
Penguin (Beijing) Ltd
7F, Tower B, Jiaming Center, 27 East Third Ring Road North,
Chaoyang District, Beijing 100020, China

Penguin Books Ltd, Registered Offices: 80 Strand, London, WC2R 0RL, England

First published by Penguin Group (Australia), 2014

1 2 3 4 5 6 7 8 9 10

Text copyright © Emusic Pty Ltd, 1990
Illustrations copyright © Mitch Vane, 2014

The moral right of the author has been asserted.

Cover and text design by Marina Messiha © Penguin Group (Australia)
Colour separation by Splitting Image Colour Studio, Clayton, Victoria
Printed and bound in China by Hung Hing Off-Set Printing, Co., Ltd

National Library of Australia
Cataloguing-in-Publication data:

Williamson, John, 1945–, author.
John Williamson's Christmas in Australia/John Williamson; Mitch Vane, illustrator.

ISBN: 978 0 670 07772 4 (hbk.)

Christmas stories, Australian. Families – Australia – Juvenile fiction

A823.3

johnwilliamson.com.au

puffin.com.au